EASTON AREA PUBLIC LIB.

3 1901 00399 7501

NO LONGER PROPERTY
OF EASTON AREA
PUBLIC LIBRARY

P9-CBK-794

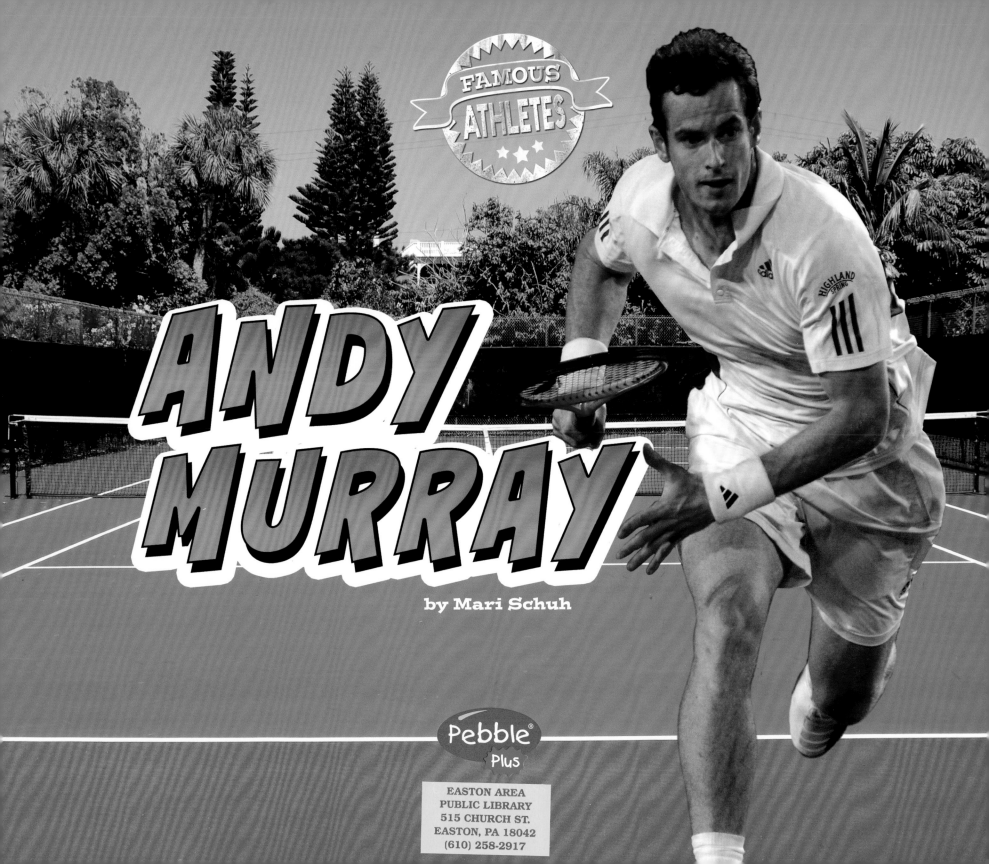

FAMOUS
ATHLETES

ANDY
MURRAY

by Mari Schuh

Pebble®
Plus

EASTON AREA
PUBLIC LIBRARY
515 CHURCH ST.
EASTON, PA 18042
(610) 258-2917

Pebble Plus is published by Capstone Press,
1710 Roe Crest Drive, North Mankato, Minnesota 56003
www.capstonepub.com

Copyright © 2016 by Capstone Press, a Capstone imprint. All rights reserved. No part of
this publication may be reproduced in whole or in part, or stored in a retrieval system, or
transmitted in any form or by any means, electronic, mechanical, photocopying, recording,
or otherwise, without written permission of the publisher.

Library of Congress Cataloging-in-Publication Data
Cataloging-in-publication information is on file with the Library of Congress.

ISBN 978-1-4914-8507-1 (hardcover)
ISBN 978-1-4914-8527-9 (paperback)
ISBN 978-1-4914-8523-1 (eBook PDF)

Editorial Credits
Gina Kammer, editor; Heidi Thompson, designer; Eric Gohl, media researcher;
Lori Barbeau, production specialist

Photo Credits
Getty Images: Clive Brunskill, 9, 11, Craig Prentis, 5, Stringer/Sara Wolfram, 13; Newscom:
Reuters/Jeff J Mitchel, 7, Reuters/Stefan Wermuth, 17, Sipa USA/Dubreuil Corinne/Abaca
Press, 21, ZUMA Press/Adam Davy, 19; Shutterstock: FlashStudio, 1, Lev Radin, cover, Neale
Cousland, 15

Design Elements: Shutterstock

To Jill—MS

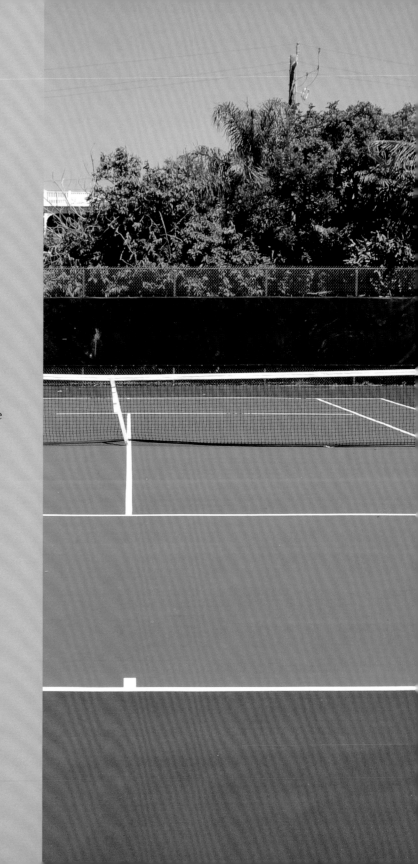

Note to Parents and Teachers

The Famous Athletes set supports national curriculum standards for social studies
related to people, places, and culture. This book describes and illustrates Andy
Murray. The images support early readers in understanding the text. The repetition
of words and phrases helps early readers learn new words. This book also introduces
early readers to subject-specific vocabulary words, which are defined in the Glossary
section. Early readers may need assistance to read some words and to use the Table of
Contents, Glossary, Read More, Internet Sites, Critical Thinking Using the Common
Core, and Index sections of the book.

Printed and bound in China.
009228S16

TABLE OF CONTENTS

BORN TO PLAY TENNIS

Tennis star Andy Murray was born
May 15, 1987. When he was 3,
he hit tennis balls with his mom.
At age 5, Andy played in his
first tournament.

1987

born in
Dunblane,
Scotland

Young Andy loved sports. He often played tennis with his brother, Jamie. Andy also played soccer. At age 15, he quit soccer to play more tennis.

1987

born in
Dunblane,
Scotland

Andy (on left) and his brother team up together to play tennis.

YOUNG CHAMPION

Andy then moved to Spain to train.

He learned how to be a better player.

Andy's hard work paid off.

In 2004 he won the U.S. Open

junior title.

1987

born in
Dunblane,
Scotland

2004

wins
U.S. Open
junior title

In 2005 Andy made history.

At age 17, he became the youngest

British player to play in the Davis Cup.

Then Andy turned pro.

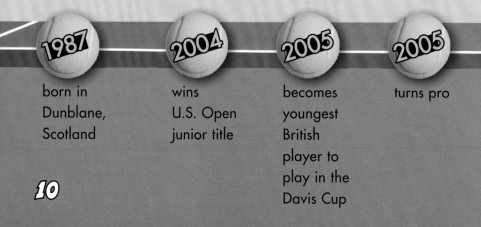

1987
born in
Dunblane,
Scotland

2004
wins
U.S. Open
junior title

2005
becomes
youngest
British
player to
play in the
Davis Cup

2005
turns pro

Andy plays in the Davis Cup.

TENNIS STAR

Andy won his first

pro tournament in 2006.

In 2008 he played in

the final of the U.S. Open.

It was his first Grand Slam final.

The Grand Slam tournaments are the top four tennis tournaments.

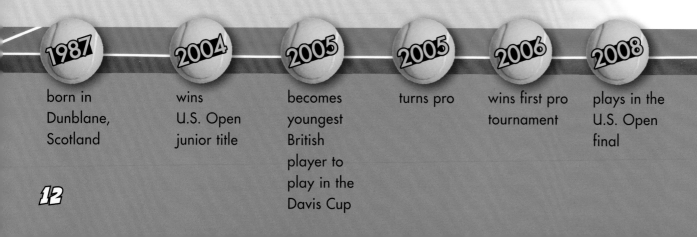

1987
born in
Dunblane,
Scotland

2004
wins
U.S. Open
junior title

2005
becomes
youngest
British
player to
play in the
Davis Cup

2005
turns pro

2006
wins first pro
tournament

2008
plays in the
U.S. Open
final

Andy lifted weights more often.

He got bigger and stronger.

In 2010 and 2011 he played in the final

of the Australian Open. Andy also made it

to the semifinals of the 2011 French Open.

1987
born in
Dunblane,
Scotland

2004
wins
U.S. Open
junior title

2005
becomes
youngest
British
player to
play in the
Davis Cup

2005
turns pro

2006
wins first pro
tournament

2008
plays in the
U.S. Open
final

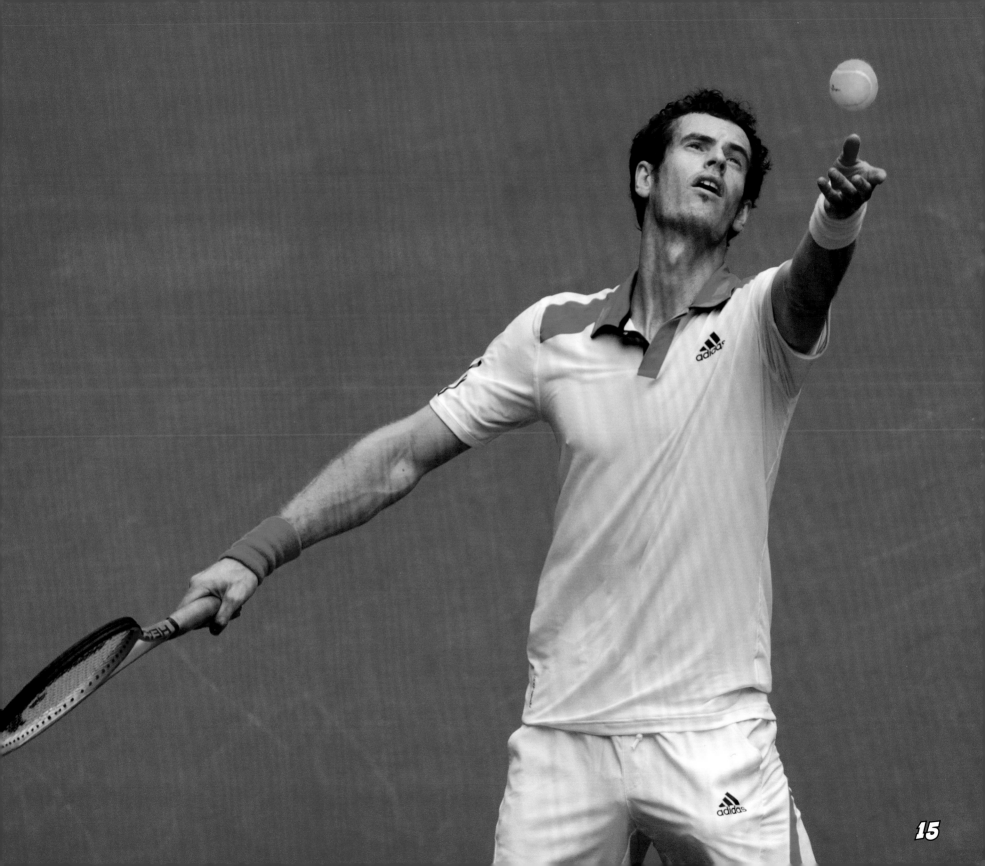

Andy enjoyed a big year in 2012.

He won a gold medal in the Olympics.

Then he won the U.S. Open. Andy

was the first man to win both events

in the same year.

1987 born in Dunblane, Scotland

2004 wins U.S. Open junior title

2005 becomes youngest British player to play in the Davis Cup

2005 turns pro

2006 wins first pro tournament

2008 plays in the U.S. Open final

2012 wins gold medal at the Olympics. Andy wins U.S. Open.

Andy soon made history again.

In 2013 he won the Wimbledon title.

Wimbledon is played in Britain.

He was the first British man

to win Wimbledon in 77 years.

1987
born in Dunblane, Scotland

2004
wins U.S. Open junior title

2005
becomes youngest British player to play in the Davis Cup

2005
turns pro

2006
wins first pro tournament

2008
plays in the U.S. Open final

2012
wins gold medal at the Olympics. Andy wins U.S. Open.

2013
wins Wimbledon

In 2015 Andy reached the final
of the Australian Open. He is one
of the world's best tennis players.
Andy wants to be a tennis star
for many more years.

1987
born in
Dunblane,
Scotland

2004
wins
U.S. Open
junior title

2005
becomes
youngest
British
player to
play in the
Davis Cup

2005
turns pro

2006
wins first pro
tournament

2008
plays in the
U.S. Open
final

2012
wins gold
medal at the
Olympics.
Andy wins
U.S. Open.

2013
wins
Wimbledon

2015
reaches
Australian
Open final

GLOSSARY

British—people from the United Kingdom; the United Kingdom is made up of England, Scotland, Wales, and Northern Ireland

Davis Cup—a men's tennis tournament played by teams from around the world

final—a match that decides the winner of a tournament

Grand Slam—the top four tennis tournaments; the Grand Slam is made up of the Australian Open, the French Open, the U.S. Open, and Wimbledon

Olympics—a competition of many sports events held every four years in a different country; people from around the world compete against one another

semifinals—two matches that decide which players play in the final

title—an award given to the winner of a tournament

tournament—a series of matches between several players, ending in one winner

train—to get ready by learning and practicing new skills

READ MORE

Bussiere, Desiree. *Tennis By the Numbers*. Minneapolis: Abdo, 2014.

Egart, Patricia. *Let's Play Tennis!: A Guide for Parents and Kids by Andy Ace*. 2nd ed. Eagan, Minn.: Amber Skye Publishing, 2013.

Morey, Allan. *Tennis*. I Love Sports. Minneapolis: Jump!, 2015.

INTERNET SITES

FactHound offers a safe, fun way to find Internet sites related to this book. All of the sites on FactHound have been researched by our staff.

Here's all you do:

Visit *www.facthound.com*

Type in this code: 9781491485071

Super-cool stuff!

Check out projects, games and lots more at
www.capstonekids.com

CRITICAL THINKING
USING THE COMMON CORE

1. What did Andy do to become a better tennis player? How did his hard work help him? (Key Ideas and Details)

2. How would Andy's life have been different if he had chosen to play soccer instead of tennis? How might his life have been the same? (Integration of Knowledge and Ideas)

3. What was one of Andy's biggest victories? Why do you think this was important for Andy? (Key Ideas and Details)

INDEX